IN THE

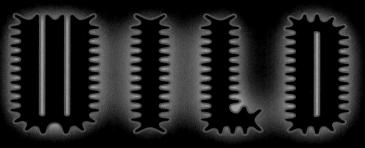

WILD

BY SNEED B. COLLARD III

Marshall Cavendish
Benchmark
New York

To Mollie, Craig, Graham, and Hayes,
For friendship, zoo adventures,
and wild golf cart rides.
—Sneed

THANK YOU!

I would not have been able to write this book without the huge help of the many kind scientists and staff associated with Zoo Atlanta. Big thanks to Dr. Terry Maple, Dr. Mollie Bloomsmith, Dr. Tara Stoinski, Dr. Thomas Butynski, Debra Forthman, and Tammie Bettinger. Extra special thanks to Graham, Hayes, and Craig Bloomsmith, avid zoo boosters.

Marshall Cavendish Benchmark
99 White Plains Road
Tarrytown, New York 10591-9001
www.marshallcavendish.us

Library of Congress Cataloging-in-Publication Data
Collard, Sneed B.
In the wild / by Sneed B. Collard III.
p. cm. — (Science adventures)
Summary: "Describes the work of Dr. Tara Stoinski, Dr. Thomas Butynski, and other zoo
biologists dedicated to saving earth's endangered species"—Provided by publisher.
Includes bibliographical references and index.
ISBN 0-7614-1955-1
1. Primates—Conservation—Juvenile literature. 2. Primatologists—Georgia—Atlanta—Juvenile literature.
3. Zoo Atlanta—Juvenile literature. I. Title.
QL737.P9C63 2005   2004031100

Series design by Anne Scatto / PIXEL PRESS

Art program assembled by Rose Corbett Gordon, Art Editor, and Alexandra Gordon, Mystic CT from the following sources.
FRONT COVER IMAGE: Cyril Ruoso /Peter Arnold, Inc. BACK COVER: Ed Degginger/Animals Animals Pages i, 32: Martin Harvey/Corbis; pages iv, 14, 44: Sneed B. Collard, III; page 2: Charles Krebs/Corbis; page 5: Mary Evans/Photo Researchers, Inc.; page 6: Reuters/Corbis; page 7: Juan M. Sanchez & Jose L. De Lope/Animals Animals; page 8: Gary W. Carter/Corbis; pages 10, 11: Kevin Schafer/Corbis; page 13: Spencer Grant/PhotoEdit; page 16: Tom & Pat Leeson/Photo Researchers, Inc.; pages 19, 30: Martin Harvey/Peter Arnold, Inc.; pages 21: W.K. Fletcher/Photo Researchers, Inc.; page 23: Carey Alan/Corbis Sygma; page 24: Martin Harvey/Photo Researchers, Inc.; pages 26, 29: Art Wolfe/Photo Researchers, Inc.; page 27: Tom Butynski; page 28: Joe McDonald/Corbis; page 34: Raoul Slater/WWI/Peter Arnold, Inc.; page 35: Michel Gunther/Peter Arnold, Inc.; page 36: Miriam Silverstein/Animals Animals; 37: Connie Bransilver/Photo Researchers, Inc.

Printed in Malaysia
135642

FRONT COVER: The future of mountain gorillas and many other of our planet's endangered species may well depend on the efforts of zoos.
BACK COVER: This emerald tree boa is only one of millions of species at risk from the destruction of tropical forests.
TITLE PAGE: Zoo scientists have taken a special interest in studying primates such as this Zanzibar red colobus monkey.

Contents

Introduction

Humans are only beginning to understand the richness and complexity of life on Earth. Every day, scientists are making new, startling discoveries about the wonderful planet we call home. The SCIENCE ADVENTURES series seeks to share the lives and adventures of a few of these scientists as they probe the mysteries of places as diverse as coral reefs, rain forests, and the deep sea.

This book focuses on a new breed of scientist: one who works in zoos. Over the past couple hundred years, zoos have evolved from being places to display unusual animals to institutions dedicated to animal conservation and public education. A small number of zoos, though, have set their goals even higher. At Zoo Atlanta, in Georgia, scientists such as Dr. Tara Stoinski and Dr. Thomas Butynski have been sent out into the wild to save our endangered primates. In doing so, they have also fashioned a new vision for the role of zoos in our planet's future.

OPPOSITE: Dr. Tara Stoinski has spearheaded Zoo Atlanta's program to save golden lion tamarins.

Amazing Monkeys and Changing Zoos

R. TARA STOINSKI WALKED through the Brazilian coastal forest, only a couple of hours from the city of Rio de Janeiro. In the forest, exotic birds called while strange insects fluttered and crawled between fabulous trees. But Tara's eyes focused on only one thing: a group of golden lion tamarins moving from branch to branch thirty feet above the ground.

The beautiful orange monkeys were part of a decades-long project to increase the population of the tamarins by reintroducing them into the wild. Tara had come to Brazil to collect data about the tamarins that would help her understand how well the program was working. As she walked, Tara carried a clipboard to keep track of exactly what the monkeys were doing. She paused frequently to take notes about the animals' behaviors.

OPPOSITE: A native of Brazil, the golden lion tamarin is one of Earth's most beautiful—and threatened—primates.

Suddenly, the tamarins stopped moving and began making agitated chirping sounds. Tara had never seen them do this before, and at first she couldn't figure out what was happening. Then she spotted a large boa constrictor on a tree branch. Instead of running away, the monkeys surrounded the snake. They called loudly to each other and made sure that each member of their group knew where the snake was.

Tara looked on excitedly. What would the tamarins do? Would they attack the snake? Would they run away?

The tamarins did neither. They stayed close to the snake, chirping to each other and moving their heads back and forth. Tara thought the boa might attack, but instead, it grew tired of all this attention. It left its perch in the branches and slithered down toward the ground. The tamarins watched it go and then continued moving through the forest.

From Gladiators to Gorillas

Tara Stoinski is a biologist who focuses on primates. That's not unusual. What is unusual is that she doesn't work for a university or a government agency. She works for a zoo. She, in fact, is helping to change not only how people think about zoos but how zoos think about themselves.

Collections of live animals, or zoos, have been around for thousands of years. Until recently, Dr. Terry Maple was the director of Zoo Atlanta and Tara Stoinski's boss. In his book *Zoo Man,* he writes, "Zoos of sorts began as far back as 2500 B.C. The ancient Greeks, like

Aristotle, kept collections of wild animals brought back by army expeditions, and the ancient Romans acquired huge collections of lions, tigers, elephants, and other wild species . . . using many of them in their warlike gladiator games."

Most of these early animal collections were in private hands, used for the enjoyment of the rich and powerful. In the eighteenth and nineteenth centuries, though, public zoos began to open across Europe and the United States. Like earlier zoos, their main purpose was entertainment. People came to zoos to look at strange or interesting animals. How the animals were cared for or what their lives were like in the wild didn't matter. They were displayed or used solely to amuse people.

However, this narrow role for zoos began changing in the late twentieth century. As scientists started to learn more about animals and as people started to care about our environment, zoos became more involved in education and conservation.

Until the late twentieth century, zoos were mostly devoted to entertainment, not the welfare of captive animals.

As zoos have become more interested in conservation, they have worked to create more natural homes for their animal residents. This tiger lives in a three-acre habitat at the Bronx Zoo in New York City.

The San Diego Zoo, for instance, began removing animals from their cramped, dreary cages and placing them in larger, more natural enclosures. The San Diego Zoo and other zoos also began educating the public about wildlife and began breeding rare and endangered animals to prevent them from going extinct. The Wildlife Conservation Society (which runs the Bronx Zoo) even gave money to support conservation efforts in Africa and other places.

Still, for Terry Maple and a handful of other zoo leaders, one part of the zoo vision was still missing: scientific research.

Zoo-volution

Zoos have a natural interest in conservation, Terry Maple explains. After all, many endangered species live in zoos, and zoos feel they should support the protection of animals in the wild. But few zoos have actually hired scientists to go out into the wild to study the animals in their natural habitats. Terry and others would like to see that change.

Studying animals in the wild as well as in zoos is the goal of Terry Maple's "zoo-volution."

Terry envisions whole teams of scientists working directly for zoos. These scientists would be out learning about wild animals. They would gain knowledge about the animals and how to protect them. "Then," Terry says, "conservation becomes a part of who we are. To me, that's the revolution that needs to be won."

Terry Maple has been working to help this "zoo-volution" move forward. When he became the director of Zoo Atlanta in 1984, he worked on developing the zoo's own scientific research program. He hired a research staff that included Tara Stoinski and other scientists who studied animals not just in the zoo, but in South America, Africa, and beyond. A special focus of this research program was primates.

Primate Professionals

OO ATLANTA'S FOCUS ON PRIMATES grew from several sources. One was Terry Maple's own scientific background. Terry earned his PhD at the University of California at Davis, studying the behavior of rhesus monkeys, baboons, and other primates. Afterward, he continued working on primates at the world-famous Yerkes National Primate Research Center at Emory University in Atlanta.

When he became director of Zoo Atlanta, Terry formed a partnership between the zoo and Yerkes. One of Terry's first goals was to build a giant, modern gorilla habitat at the zoo. This habitat became home to thirteen gorillas that had been living at Yerkes, as well as one male gorilla who had already been living at the zoo.

Terry also began building a scientific research team that included many primate experts. These experts began conducting studies on

OPPOSITE: A partnership between Zoo Atlanta and the Yerkes research center led to the creation of the zoo's world-class gorilla habitat.

primates within Zoo Atlanta. The zoo also became involved in a variety of projects to support conservation research in the field. One of these was the golden lion tamarin reintroduction project.

Tails of Woe

Golden lion tamarins are small, beautiful orange monkeys that inhabit the coastal Atlantic forests of Brazil. Their forest homes are not nearly as famous as Brazil's Amazonian rain forests, but they are much more endangered. Since Europeans began settling in Brazil almost five hundred years ago, more than 93 percent of these coastal

The golden lion tamarin reintroduction project was a natural fit for Zoo Atlanta's team of biologists.

Hikers cross a bridge in a forest along Brazil's coast. Nearly all of these Atlantic forests have been destroyed, leading to the decline of the golden lion tamarin and many other species.

forests have been cleared for farms, pastures, and other uses. This forest loss has been devastating for wildlife, including the golden lion tamarin.

By the early 1970s, only 100 to 200 golden lion tamarins survived in the wild. Another 30 lived in captivity in Brazil, and about 80 lived in zoos worldwide. Conservationists realized that to save the species, they needed to act fast. In 1973, the Brazilian government established a reserve to protect the tamarins' habitat. Zoos around the world also stepped up breeding programs to increase the number of tamarins in captivity.

In 1984 scientists at the National Zoo in Washington, DC, began a program to reintroduce some of the captive-bred tamarins back into the wild. Eventually, six U.S. zoos—including Zoo Atlanta—began raising golden lion tamarins for release back into Brazil. The problem was that the reintroductions weren't very successful. The tamarins didn't adapt well to their new wild Brazilian homes, and 70 percent died within their first year.

Tamarin Boot Camp

To improve survival, scientists at the National Zoo began trying to train the tamarins before their release. They hid food in the tamarins' cages to make the monkeys look for it, as they might in a natural forest. They created different travel routes that resembled connections of forest tree branches. The training didn't seem to help. When they were released in Brazil, most of the tamarins didn't begin foraging and exploring like wild tamarins. Instead, they just hung around the spots where they were released.

But this gave scientists another idea. "Since tamarins naturally like to stay in one area," the scientists asked themselves, "why don't we actually release them in the zoos as if they lived in the wild?"

In 1986, the National Zoo released a group of tamarins in an "open exhibit" full of trees and other plants. The tamarins had a home box—a converted ice chest—to live in, but were free to explore and wander anywhere in the zoo. Fortunately, the tamarins stayed in a pretty small area, as they would in the wild. Soon, the five other zoos—including Zoo Atlanta—also began placing their tamarins in open exhibits.

Over the next decade, all of the tamarins that were released in Brazil were first trained in open "boot camps" in zoos. These open exhibits were very popular with the zoo-going public, and scientists hoped they would improve tamarin survival in the wild. Still, no one knew if they really did. When the tamarins were released, some groups did better than others, but no one knew why.

Enter Tara Stoinski.

Predicting Success

Tara Stoinski grew up in New Jersey, close to the city of Philadelphia. "My family was always very interested in animals," Tara recalls. "My mother loves animals and my dad does as well. So like every other little kid that really likes animals, I wanted to be a veterinarian."

Zoo Atlanta director Terry Maple hired Tara Stoinski to join his
field research team.

For her undergraduate college degree, though, Tara decided to study
history. It wasn't until she earned her master's degree in biology at
Oxford University that she began studying science in earnest. By this
time, she'd decided against becoming a vet and, instead, pursued a
career in biology. After her master's degree, she spent time working with
jackals in Africa. Then, in 1994, Terry Maple hired Tara as a senior
research associate at Zoo Atlanta. Meanwhile, Tara also began her PhD
work at the Georgia Institute of Technology and was shopping around
for a PhD research project. During this "shopping expedition," she met
a man named Benjamin Beck, who coordinates the tamarin reintroduction program for the National Zoo.

Ben wanted someone to develop a way to evaluate tamarins *before* they were sent to Brazil. He especially wanted a way to predict how well a tamarin might do in the wild by watching its behavior beforehand. Ben thought such a behavioral test might increase the success rate of the reintroductions. It would also reduce the expense of the program, since each tamarin that was released cost about $22,000 to raise, transport, release, and watch during its lifetime.

When they met, Ben asked Tara if she might be interested in developing such a behavioral test. Tara jumped at the chance.

Tamarin Testing

VER THE NEXT YEAR, Tara began pinpointing a set of behaviors that people could use to evaluate tamarins before they were reintroduced into the wild. In looking at several groups of captive tamarins, Tara found that they behaved very differently. One group of tamarins that lived at Zoo Atlanta, for instance, was very active. "They were doing everything," Tara says. "They were running around, they were searching for food, they were interacting with the environment and even chasing squirrels. Another group at the National Zoo, on the other hand, spent 60 percent of their time in their shelter. They basically didn't do very much."

Not surprisingly, when these two groups were released into the wild, the Atlanta group did much better than the National Zoo group. Tara

OPPOSITE: The low success rate of early golden lion tamarin releases led to one of Tara's first research projects: to try to predict which animals would do better in the wild.

felt that she was close to being able to predict how to choose which tamarins would do best when they were reintroduced—and dramatically improve the success of the reintroduction program.

However, soon after Tara began working on her evaluation list, the reintroduction program slowed down. "Basically," Tara explains, "they ran out of habitat for reintroducing new animals." At first, Tara was disappointed by this. But soon she started working on another tamarin project that was even more interesting—and, perhaps, even more important.

Leaving the "Ark"

One dream of conservationists is that someday many species of endangered animals can be reintroduced back into the wild. The idea is to protect these species within zoos or other "arks" until there are again safe places for them to live in the wild. Then they will be set free.

The reasons for this dream are obvious. All around the world, human activities are destroying animal habitats. Forests are being cut down for logs or to create pastures. Coral reefs are being killed by coastal development and global warming. Prairies, deserts, and chaparral are being swallowed up by growing cities. For many species, zoos are becoming their last refuge for survival.

However, in some cases—including those of the golden lion tamarin, California condor, and black-footed ferret—biologists have already been able to reintroduce animals back into the wild.

"Since the year 1900," Tara explains, "over thirteen million animals have been reintroduced. The vast majority are reptiles and fish. There

hasn't been a ton of mammals or birds reintroduced. But we probably only have data on survival rates of maybe twenty thousand of these thirteen million. Unfortunately, it's not a very sci-

Over the years, many animals, like these orphaned western gorillas, have been reintroduced into the wild. Tara's project, though, was one of the first to closely examine how animals fare after they are released.

entific endeavor. People tend to release the animals and say 'Oh, they did well' or 'Oh, they died.' No one has really looked at their behavior. So if these reintroduced animals are dying, no one's asked what it is about their behavior that's lacking. They haven't looked at how these animals adapt to their environment and how their offspring adapt."

With the golden lion tamarins, though, Tara recognized an opportunity to help fill in some missing information about animal reintroductions.

Digging Through Data

What Tara and Ben Beck realized was that the golden lion tamarin project had collected almost twenty years of good data on tamarin releases. Since the reintroductions began in 1984, dozens of people in Brazil had been following the tamarin groups, recording what and how they were doing.

"So Ben and I started talking," Tara explains. "We said, 'Here's an incredible opportunity. There's probably no database like this in the world and it's not being used. Wouldn't it be neat to know what these animals are doing, how their offspring are adapting, and how many generations it takes tamarins to behave like wild tamarins?'"

They decided that yes, it would be neat. So in 1998, Tara went to Brazil to observe tamarins in the forest. She also began entering years of older tamarin data into the computer. What did she find out?

Tamarin Testimonies

Tara basically learned that captive-born adult tamarins may not ever totally adapt to the wild. Their abilities to find food and move through the trees improve over time, but even after two years, they need a lot of help from people to survive.

Tara, though, found other fascinating facts. One was that juvenile tamarins that are released into the wild (with their parents) adapt more quickly than their parents do. This suggests that reintroducing animals when they're younger may increase their survival rates.

Tara's findings grew even more interesting when she examined the *offspring* of reintroduced tamarins. Tara discovered that the first generation of tamarins born in Brazil still don't totally adapt to the wild. They move and forage more effectively than their reintroduced parents do, but not as well as offspring of wild tamarins. Tara believes this is because an animal's behavior depends on both its environment *and* its social circumstances. Since the first generation of offspring have parents that are not very skilled at living in the wild, those

At a reintroduction feeding station in Brazil, a golden lion tamarin makes a meal of bananas.

offspring don't learn as well as they could from wild parents. On the other hand, they are learning much more from their environment than their parents ever did.

But the story doesn't stop there.

The Super Survivors

"Where it gets interesting," Tara says, "is when those same captive-born parents have babies again. That second set of babies are now being raised by their parents *and* by their older brothers and sisters who were born in Brazil. And now we see a very large difference. This second set of offspring behaves somewhat differently from their older siblings, but they are *very* different from their parents. So while the first offspring develop pretty good skills, it's the second set of offspring that really takes off."

The success of tamarin offspring, in fact, is a big reason reintroductions have slowed down in Brazil. Over the past decade or two, the overall population of wild tamarins has increased to about 1,000 animals. Now, when a new habitat opens up in Brazil, scientists can fill that space with offspring from previous reintroductions.

Tara's research provides a valuable tool for other wildlife managers hoping to do animal reintroductions. Instead of just throwing the animals out into the wild and hoping they'll survive, the golden lion tamarin project has shown how important it is to watch over and support the first generation of animals that is released. By helping animals that are reintroduced, you improve the chances that they will have off-

spring that can survive much better in the wild. Tara's data, however, also show how difficult it can be to reintroduce animals into the wild at all—a warning to people who believe that zoos can save all endangered wild species.

Many kinds of animals, including other tamarin species, can benefit from Tara's research in the field.

CHAPTER 4

Apes in Trouble

THE TAMARIN PROJECT IS not the only scientific field program Zoo Atlanta has supported. In 1993, the zoo launched its Africa Biodiversity Conservation Program. The goal of the program was to support projects that help people learn about and conserve African *biodiversity*—the number and variety of wild species in Africa—especially threatened primates and birds. Dr. Thomas Butynski was appointed the program's first senior conservation biologist.

Tom Butynski grew up on a farm in western Massachusetts in the town of Greenfield. "There were, and still are, a lot of large fields, brooks, woods, and swamps around," Tom explains. "We raised cows for milk, chickens for eggs, and crops to sell in the surrounding towns. We also had time to play sports, play in the fields and woods, go swimming and fishing, bird watching, and hunting."

OPPOSITE: Chimpanzees and other apes are a special focus of Zoo Atlanta's wildlife conservation program.

Dr. Tom Butynski first studied apes in the dense tropical forests of western Uganda.

Tom's early exposure to nature led to a lifelong passion for wildlife and conservation. "I first went to Africa in 1970 to work for three and a half years as a Peace Corps volunteer for the Botswana Department of Tourism, Wildlife, and National Parks," he recalls. "After Botswana, I began work in the tropical forests of western Uganda, studying gorillas and working to conserve these forests."

Along the way, Tom earned a PhD from Michigan State University and became one of the world's top experts in finding and identifying a wide variety of African animals, especially mammals and birds.

Hooo's Out There?

A large part of Tom's work focuses on simply finding out what lives in Africa's wild places. Despite the fame of Africa's "big game" animals, many parts of Africa are still scientific mysteries.

"The areas I survey are always very poorly known biologically," Tom explains. "In many cases, no previous biological surveys have been conducted in the areas."

To help correct this situation, Tom often joins teams of other biologists who are experts on plants, reptiles, amphibians, insects, and other living things. These teams go out into forests and other areas that are thought to have large numbers of threatened species and *endemic species*—species that live only in particular places.

On these surveys, Tom slowly walks along trails and roads searching for primates and other large mammals and

A major focus of Tom's work is simply documenting what animals live in Africa's wild places. While working in the Itombwe Mountains near Lake Tanganyika, for instance, Tom became the first person to ever capture and photograph the Congo Bay Owl. He released it a few minutes after he snapped this picture.

27

birds. He also looks for signs of human activities. Since he often works in dense forests, he has learned to identify many animals by their calls or sounds. He records everything he finds, and his information is used by conservation agencies and African officials to identify and protect places that are especially important to wild species.

Tom's surveys typically last about a month, and they've led to some amazing discoveries. In the Itombwe Mountains near Lake Tanganyika, Tom rediscovered two species of birds that hadn't been seen for forty years. One was a nightjar and the other was an owl. He was the first person ever to record the call of the nightjar and to photograph the owl.

Tom's most urgent findings, however, have to do with primates.

The western gorilla is one of four species of great apes that live in Africa.

Land of the Apes

Scientists consider Africa to be the cradle of primate evolution. Our human ancestors may have been evolving in Africa as long as seven million years ago. Today, Africa is home to four of Earth's six species of great apes: the robust chimpanzee (also called the common chimpanzee), the gracile chimpanzee (also called the pygmy chimpanzee or bonobo), the western gorilla, and the eastern gorilla. Only two species of great apes—two kinds of orangutans—make their home outside of Africa, in Southeast Asia.

Unfortunately, all of Earth's great apes are in big trouble. In the past two decades, Africa's human population has more than doubled. Many wildlands have been converted to farms and grazing areas. Africa is also the poorest continent on Earth. To survive, many African people hunt and eat wild animals of all kinds, from birds to primates. They also destroy forests for fuel wood and building materials.

To make matters worse, logging companies from Asia, Europe, and North America have been pushing into Africa's tropical forests, cutting down trees and building roads to places that used to be wild and inaccessible. These new roads have allowed in a flood of hunters, and the slaughter of wild animals—or "bushmeat"—has devastated Africa's mammals, birds, and reptiles.

Only a fraction of Africa's gorilla populations survive today.

Africa's four ape species have been especially hard-hit. Many ape populations have disappeared from places where forests have been destroyed or fragmented into patches that are too small to support them. Bushmeat hunters have taken an even greater toll. Hunters especially target apes because they are big and provide a lot of meat. The hunters sell ape meat to loggers and people living in cities hundreds of miles away. Finding out just how many apes survive is a gigantic task, but one of Tom's missions is to try.

Bushmeat hunters have devastated Africa's wildlife. Apes and other primates have been especially hard-hit.

Counting Apes

To get an idea of how many great apes are left, Tom collects information from dozens of people working in Africa. Tom also gathers data himself during his wildlife surveys, and he visits markets around Africa to count ape carcasses. What has he found?

Tom estimates that robust chimpanzees—the most populous of Africa's apes—have a population of about 187,000 in Africa. He also estimates that there are about 40,000 gracile chimpanzees, 94,000 western gorillas, and about 17,000 eastern gorillas. These numbers may sound like a lot, but they are only a fraction of the numbers that used to live in Africa. Chimpanzee expert Jane Goodall, for instance, estimates that more than 2 million robust chimpanzees once lived in Africa—ten times today's population.

"Africa is losing its forests faster than any other continent," Tom writes in a recent magazine article. "Only six countries have more than 20 per cent of their original forest cover remaining, while as many as 17 countries retain less than 10 per cent. . . . Logging in Africa is almost always an unmanaged, uncontrolled and unsustainable activity that often represents the first step in a series of events that end in the obliteration of the forest and its apes."

From their work, Tom and other African-primate experts conclude "that chimpanzee and gorilla numbers are in sharp decline in the wild, that the rate of decline is rapidly accelerating, and that all four species will become extinct in the wild if the causal factors are not sufficiently addressed."

In other words, if people don't take radical steps to protect these animals and improve the situations of African people, the four ape species are doomed.

CHAPTER 5

Zoos in the Spotlight

THE WORK OF TARA STOINSKI, Tom Butynski, and other zoo wildlife scientists shines a spotlight on the importance of biological research—and the benefits of having zoos involved in this research. We live in a time when animals, their habitats, and nature itself are under attack from almost every direction. Scientists estimate that Earth is home to between 10 and 100 million species of living things. And yet, every year, thousands of animal and plant species are going extinct as we destroy the forests, reefs, and other places where they live.

Biological research not only helps us understand and appreciate what we are losing—it provides us with the information we need to save species. When the golden lion tamarin project began, for example, a big problem was that zoos couldn't get the monkeys to breed in captivity. The key turned out to be how the tamarins were being kept. In the wild,

OPPOSITE: The field research of zoo scientists can provide information essential for saving many species of wildlife. Here Dr. Mike Loomis of the North Carolina Zoological Park conducts a study of elephants in Cameroon.

most primates live in groups that consist of one male and several females. Zookeepers naturally assumed that's how tamarins lived, too. Then, researchers discovered that tamarins live in groups that often consist of only one breeding male and one breeding female. As soon as scientists changed the groups in the zoos, tamarin breeding took off.

Biological research also helps us identify which places we should concentrate on saving. Tom Butynski's surveys in Africa are helping governments and conservation groups target places that have the richest habitats and numbers of species.

Tom Butynski's work in Tanzania's Udzungwa Mountains showed how important the area was to nine species of primates, including the red colobus monkey.

In 1997, for example, Tom spearheaded the Udzungwa Primate Conservation Project. This project focused on surveying Tanzania's Udzungwa Mountains. Before the survey, scientists suspected that these mountains held many biological riches, but no one knew enough about them to know for sure. Tom and his colleagues gathered evidence that showed just how important the Udzungwas are—especially to the nine species of primates that live there. Of these nine species, two—the red colobus monkey and the Sanje mangabey—live only in the Udzungwas. Tom's surveys provided the Tanzanian government and international conservation groups with the information and reasons to protect the mountains and their animals.

Field research by Tom and other biologists has also raised worldwide awareness of the bushmeat crisis. Tom has written several articles about the plight of Africa's apes. He has also contributed his knowledge and expertise to the Bushmeat Crisis Task Force. This task force is a coalition of more than thirty conservation groups, agencies, and zoos working to stop the slaughter of Africa's wildlife. Together, they raise money to fund conservation activities, help train and educate Africans to stop illegal hunting, and pressure governments and industry to stop illegal logging.

Stopping the bushmeat trade is among today's highest conservation priorities.

But Why Zoos?

Still, many people continue to ask why zoos should be involved in this kind of research. Along with the Wildlife Conservation Society, Zoo Atlanta remains one of a handful of zoos that actively pursues field research. Most zoos find it impossible to support field scientists like Tom Butynski, and many people ask, why bother? Terry Maple has several answers.

"To advance the cause of the animal," Terry explains, "you have to know the animal. And you can't just know where it is and where it came from." Terry argues that you have to understand how the animal lives

in the wild and also understand the habitat it lives in. To do that, you need to have scientists out there studying these things, scientists who interact with the zoo and can make recommendations about which animals to keep and how to keep them.

The scientific research conducted by zoos helps them educate the public about animals and conservation.

Terry also argues that it's important for zoos to be the experts on animals in their care. As zoos take on a bigger role in educating the public about animals and conservation, it's essential that they have the latest scientific information. "Yesterday's information isn't good enough," Terry says. He believes zoos have to be directly involved with scientists who are gathering cutting-edge data about animal behavior, biology, and conservation.

Only by having this firsthand scientific knowledge will zoos be taken seriously by the public that supports them. Animal rights groups often criticize zoos, aquariums, and similar institutions for not treating their animals with the care and respect they deserve. In the past, such criticisms were often justified. Scientific research, though, has allowed many zoos to keep their animals in conditions that are as close to their natural habitats as possible. This ends up better for the animals—and better for the public that goes to see and learn about them.

Conservation: A Joint Effort

Terry, however, does not see zoos as a substitute for wilderness. He explains: "It would be very easy to say, 'This creature can only live in zoos and will never be able to survive in the wild.' But I don't want the zoo to be the last refuge for endangered species. If it is, we've failed."

Terry and many others believe that if we can't save species in the wild, many of those species will disappear, even if some are temporarily protected in zoos. Part of the reason has to do with *inbreeding*—having a population so

Though zoos may be able to save certain species, thousands—perhaps millions—of other species will become extinct if we cannot protect their natural habitats.

small that it doesn't have the genetic variation to allow it to survive. For instance, the mountain gorilla (a subspecies of the eastern gorilla) has a population of only about 350 animals. "If that were to get dramatically smaller," Terry says, "you might not be able to save them even if you plucked them out of the wild."

Also, Terry asks, if you ever could return endangered animals to the wild, what would you be sending them back to? How would they survive in an environment that's not only altered, but completely different from the one that they're used to in the zoo?

For these and other reasons, Terry believes that zoos should join forces with other conservation groups, governments, and the public to fight the destruction of wild habitats. Zoo Atlanta is taking part by supporting the Bushmeat Crisis Task Force and other conservation programs. Other zoos have gotten involved, too.

"This is a massively important issue that gets pushed aside when you're at war with terrorists or whatever else we're doing in the world," Terry says. "But we have to recognize that we're waging a bigger war, the war we have with ourselves to protect the world we live in and the good green earth that sustains every living thing. This is a huge, huge conflict, and if we don't resolve it in a positive way, we'll all be in trouble."

Glossary

ADAPT to change in a way that allows an organism to survive better

BIODIVERSITY the total number of species on Earth; the total number of habitats on Earth; and the sum of genetic diversity in Earth's species

COALITION a team with common goals or purposes

CONSERVATION the protection of Earth's natural resources, such as its wildlife, forests, and rivers

DATA measurements and other information collected by scientists

DATABASE a large collection of data, or information, that can be used by scientists

ENDEMIC living or existing only in a particular area; also describes something that comes from a particular area

EVOLUTION the process by which species change over time via mutations that happen in their DNA; evolution is also what creates new species from older ones

EXTINCT describes a species that has no surviving individuals, one that has disappeared from Earth forever

GENETIC VARIATION the total differences found in the genes, or DNA, of a species or other population of organisms

GLOBAL WARMING the rise in Earth's temperatures caused by carbon dioxide and other gases that trap heat in our atmosphere

HABITAT the place or environment where a plant or animal lives and grows

INBREEDING breeding, or reproducing, within a population that is too small to stay healthy because of its limited genetic variation

PhD a doctorate, or advanced degree, from a university

PRIMATE a group of mammals that includes humans, apes, and monkeys; all primates have eyes that look forward, large brains, and fingers and thumbs that can grasp things

REINTRODUCE to take captive-raised animals and release them back into wild habitats

SPECIES a group of animals or plants that have many characteristics in common; members of the same species can mate and have offspring

SUBSPECIES a population of a species that has some characteristics that differ from those of other members of the species but that is still able to interbreed with those members

UNSUSTAINABLE not able to be continued; using a resource in a way that permanently damages, or even destroys, it

To Learn More

Books

Hundreds of books have been written about tamarins, apes, zoos, and primate conservation. Interesting titles include:

Ancona, George. *The Golden Lion Tamarin Comes Home.* New York: Simon and Schuster, 1994.

Elwood, Ann. *Chimpanzees.* Poway, CA: Wildlife Education, Ltd., 2001.

Elwood, Ann. *Old World Monkeys.* Poway, CA: Wildlife Education, Ltd., 2000.

Goodall, Jane. *My Life with the Chimpanzees.* New York: Simon and Schuster, 1996.

Patent, Dorothy Hinshaw. *Back to the Wild.* San Diego: Harcourt Brace, 1997.

Wexo, John Bonnett. *Apes.* Poway, CA: Wildlife Education, Ltd., 2001.

Wexo, John Bonnett. *Gorillas.* Poway, CA: Wildlife Education, Ltd., 2003.

Web sites

For those interested in the bushmeat crisis and zoo conservation activities, look up the Web sites of the following organizations. These sites contain many links to others involved with research and conservation.

The Bushmeat Crisis Task Force. This group works to raise awareness about the bushmeat crisis and mobilize action to stem this destructive practice. Web site: www.bushmeat.org

National Zoo/Smithsonian Institution. Coordinators for the golden lion tamarin reintroduction project as well as many other conservation activities. Web site: www.nationalzoo.si.edu

Wildlife Conservation Society. A pioneer at combining zoo management with conservation, WCS manages the Bronx Zoo and is involved in a huge variety of conservation programs. Web site: www.wcs.org

Zoo Atlanta. Zoo Atlanta is involved in a variety of conservation and research projects on primates as well as pandas, reptiles, and other species. Web site: www.zooatlanta.org

Index

Page numbers for illustrations are in boldface.

About the Author

SNEED B. COLLARD III has written more than fifty books for young people. They include the popular picture books *Animal Dads, Leaving Home,* and *Animals Asleep* as well as in-depth science books such as *Monteverde: Science and Scientists in a Costa Rican Cloud Forest.* His books *The Forest in the Clouds* and *Beaks!* were both named Teacher's Choices by the International Reading Association, and many of his other titles have received similar recognition. Before beginning his writing career, Sneed graduated with honors in biology from the University of California at Berkeley. To research and photograph the SCIENCE ADVENTURES series, he visited Costa Rica's cloud forest, Australia's Great Barrier Reef, Zoo Atlanta, and the deep-sea floor. Sneed lives in Missoula, Montana, where he enjoys observing nature during long walks with his border collie, Mattie. His Web site is: www.sneedbcollardiii.com